Dr. Cassundra White-Elliott

Safety in
יהוה

"He shall cover thee with his feathers,
and under his wings shalt thou trust."
Psalm 91:4

This is a work of fiction combined with the Word of God. Any resemblance to actual occurrences is purely coincidental. Included scripture are from the King James Version of the Holy Bible.

CLF Publishing, LLC.
www.clfpublishing.org
909.315.3161

Cover design by Senir Design. Contact information: info@senirdesign.com.

ISBN # 978-1-945102-36-3

Printed in the United States of America.

INTRODUCTION

A person's disposition is an outward demonstration of his/her level of spirituality and faith. For example, a person who has weak faith or even no faith in God is easily flustered by the trials that cross his/her path. This person has a tendency to fall faint, fall into depression, commit suicide, turn to drugs, alcohol, or self-mutilation, or take other drastic measures because he/she is unable to cope with everyday life situations.

On the other end of the spectrum, someone who possesses strong or great faith is not easily moved by circumstances, trials, tribulations, or the changes that may take place in the natural. For, he/she knows a greater spiritual force is at work. This person knows he/she is able to call on God in the midst of it all *and* God will answer. Philippians 4:6-7 tells us, *"Be careful for nothing; but in everything by prayer and supplication with thanksgiving let your requests be made known unto God. And the peace of God, which passeth all understanding, shall keep your hearts and minds through Christ Jesus."*

Then the verses continue with verse 8 that says, *"Finally, brethren, whatsoever things are true, whatsoever things are honest, whatsoever things are just, whatsoever things are pure, whatsoever things are lovely, whatsoever things are of good report; if there be any virtue, and if there be any praise, think on these things."*

Here, we are reminded how we should be thinking and what we should be thinking about. If we find ourselves occupied with thoughts that are positive, we don't have time to allow our mind to be cluttered with thoughts that can traumatize us and cause us anxiety.

In this book, excerpts of a trying time in Christopher's life are shared. During this season, he is inundated with trials. How will he respond to them? What example will he provide for his son? Will the trials overtake him and weaken his resolve, or will he weather the storm?

As you read, allow the Holy Spirit to minister to you and strengthen any area in which you may be weak.

PART ONE

"He that dwelleth in the secret place of the most High
shall abide under the shadow of the Almighty."
Psalm 91:1

Ever since my wife Cindy died, nearly three years ago, things have been quite rough to say the least. Christopher Jr., whom I lovingly call CJ, is my eleven-year-old son. He is also my namesake. We were both extremely close to his mother, as we were a tight-knit family. Losing her to a drunk driver, a week after Mother's Day, was a devastating blow to both of us. If it were not for close friends, family, and church members surrounding us, I don't know how we could have remained emotionally stable.

Since her death, it has been a financial roller coaster ride. I have been trying to make ends meet month after month, while making the adjustment from a two-income household to a one-income household. In the midst of juggling jobs, I was also working hard to not to be away from my son more than necessary. He had begun to demonstrate signs of abandonment a month or so after his mother's death, so I wanted to spend as much time with him as possible, allowing my presence to reassure him.

I managed to keep a handle on the juggling act for a little while with the help of my mother who watched CJ some evenings. But her health took a turn for the worst, and I had to move her into a nursing home. Then, two months ago, I lost my full-time job. I had been working at an energy plant and had finally made it to the position of foreman after seventeen years of employment. I had twice before applied for the position but was denied for advancement.

After the lay-off, I immediately applied for unemployment benefits and qualified. I am grateful for the funds. However, my unemployment check is barely enough to put food on the table and pay the utility bills, let alone pay the rent. Nothing good could have come from not being able to pay the rent. Then, as was inevitable, an eviction notice came just days ago, stating we had three days to pay or quit.

CJ and I had already downsized from our modest home two years ago to a two-bedroom apartment. That was a difficult process. My wife and I had decided to make the purchase of a family home when she was pregnant with CJ. We completed the purchase when he was nine months old.

About six or seven months after my wife passed, reluctantly, I went through some of her belongings. However, with the move, I was forced to go through everything. The process was emotionally draining, not to mention the physical exertion of having to lift an entire household of furniture. The only person who was available to assist in the move was my wife's sister, and she is far too frail to lift heavy furniture. She was only able to manage some bags and a few small boxes.

Then quite unexpectantly, just before the heavy furniture needed to be moved, my next-door neighbor came home from work. He was surprised to see us moving out, and because we were not particularly close, I had not bothered to mention it to him. After chitchatting for a while, making idle small talk, he immediately changed his clothes and lent a hand. I was extremely grateful and so was my back.

Thankfully after the move, my son was still able to go to the same school, but the neighborhood we moved to was a little unsavory, to put it nicely. There were gang activity and drug sales on a daily basis. But, it was better than nothing. Now, we have no home to call our own. Although my son is extremely intelligent and mature for his age, it was very difficult to look him in the face and tell him we had no place to call our home. CJ took it like a trooper. He told me, "Dad, as long as we are together, we will be okay."

His words caused tears to spring from my eyes. The heaviness I had been carrying in my heart was immediately lifted. I certainly did not want to cause my son more distress. In his young life, he had gone through too much already. It was my sole responsibility to encourage him and protect him, as much as humanly possible. But, through all he had been through, he had grown stronger. So, my son was encouraging me- right at a moment that I needed it the most. I could not have been prouder at that moment, as a father, than at any other time.

Since the move, I have been living in my automobile with some of my belongings for the past couple of days. The rest of my items are in storage. Hopefully, I will be able to pay the monthly bill to avoid losing all our earthly possessions. Then, to add to the stress and heartache of the eviction, while storing all of our material items, I had to simultaneously concern myself with shelter for my son.

Due to the crunch we found ourselves in, my wife's sister has allowed CJ to live with her temporarily. And she did emphasize that her invitation was *temporary*. Although she feels for our plight and she loves her nephew dearly, she has her own problems. She and her children live in a one-bedroom apartment, with her youngest child sleeping on the couch and the oldest in a sleeping bag padded with blankets on the floor. She doesn't have any support from either of her children's father, so I am tremendously grateful she allowed my son to join the crew. The last thing I want to worry about is his physical safety. The streets are no place for a child to live, and I will do anything to ensure my son does not suffer that fate.

All of these life-changing episodes have caused me to find myself in prayer more and more these days, crying out to the Lord for direction and guidance. Don't get me wrong. I am not new to prayer or seeking the Lord's guidance. I have been a faithful follower of Christ for more than half my life. Although I haven't experienced much turmoil, with the exception of the passing of my father, in my life like I had in the last three years, forever will I trust Him.

I just seem to be praying more and more for His divine protection these days. Furthermore, I need His wisdom. I know without the Lord in my life things could be even worse. And, I can't imagine that. I trust Him explicitly and without reservation.

And even though the enemy is fighting me tooth and nail, I refuse to give up on God. Because through it all, God has not given up on me. He has been with me every step of the way, through the pain, through the tears, through the times of feeling lost, through the disappointment, through the loneliness, through the hopelessness, through it all.

I know if you are on the outside looking in, it may be hard for you to conceptualize how I view the goodness of the Lord in my life. But, He has not ever failed me. And, I don't anticipate that He ever will.

I have chosen God as my guardian, and in Him, all my needs and desires have been and will continue to be met. Although I may not have the shelter of a home with a roof and four walls, God shelters me and will come between me and anything that should annoy me, whether storm, threat, or danger. Under God's protection, He will be my rest and refuge forever.

Due to Christopher's unwavering convictions and dedication to the Lord, he can rest assured that he dwells in the secret place of the Most High. Some believers are known for continually running to the secret place, when and only when, they find themselves in trouble. On the other hand, a believer who knows the benefits of being in the mysterious presence of the Almighty will find him/herself habitually residing in God's presence, in order to obtain the benefits therein.

Understanding that the veil was rent for us upon Christ's death, revealing God's mercy seat, allows for deeper and continual communion with God and for us to become possessors of rare and special benefits, which are not received by all believers. This may be difficult for us to comprehend, knowing God is no respecter of persons. However, to receive full access to His providence, we must seek out a true and infinite relationship with Him. His arms are open, awaiting our return. We need to seek His endearing embrace.

According to Charles Spurgeon, "The Omnipotent Lord will shield all those who dwell in Him. They shall remain under His care as guests under the protection of their host. Those who commune with God are safe with Him. No evil can reach them, for the outstretched wings of His power and love cover them from all harm. This protection is constant -- they abide under it, and it is sufficient, for it is the shadow of the Almighty whose omnipotence will surely screen them from all attacks. Communion with God is safety. The more closely we cling to our Almighty Father, the more confident may we be."

PART TWO

"I will say of the Lord, He is my refuge and my fortress:
my God; in him will I trust."
Psalm 91:2

As I make myself comfortable in the backseat of my automobile and try to stay warm, I am reflecting on my day. Normally, my day begins with picking up my son from his aunt's and dropping him off at school. However, today was scheduled a tad bit differently. My son and his cousins began their winter break from school today, so I did not make my customary trip to my sister-in-law's home at seven this morning.

Instead, this morning began with an unwanted appointment at the Employment Development Department to discuss my recent job search and to obtain their assistance with job leads should they have job listings for which I am skilled. To my surprise, the meeting was actually lucrative unlike others I have been to in the past. I received two job offers once I followed up on the five leads that were provided to me. However, before I share the details of my two prospective jobs, let me share an interesting moment that occurred during my meeting.

When I informed the counselor about my son and I having been displaced from our home, she gave me the strangest look as I praised God for what He is doing in our lives despite our reality. Very politely, I asked her why she had the strange look on her face, and she replied, "I don't understand your praise and what you are excited about." I detected slight sarcasm in her voice, but I opted to ignore it because I knew there was a greater challenge in store.

So, I proceeded to ask her if she believed in God, and she responded, "To a certain extent, but I don't believe in divine purpose and miracles if that's what you're asking." I ended the brief conversation with, "Then you would _not_ understand my praise." I made that statement with a smile on my face because inside of me the joy of the Lord is full. The woman ignored my statement and proceeded on with her conversation regarding my job search and me getting work.

I did not mean any harm or disrespect toward the counselor. I just knew in the time I would spend with her, it would take more than an instant to explain my disposition. So, before I left the building, I simply told her, "God is good to me all the time. You should try Him out." She gave a slight shrug of her shoulders. It was if though she wanted to demonstrate her disbelief in the power of the Almighty. But, her response was a weak attempt to shrug God off. Deep inside, I belief she wanted to talk more about Him. I believe God will send someone her way to open the door to filling the void she has.

As for me, God promised in His Word that He would never leave me nor would He forsake me. So even though others may not understand my praise, I will yet praise the Lord.

I left the meeting in good spirits and proceeded to call the first job lead. The supervisor informed me that the position had already been filled. So, I continued to make my way down the list of leads, and I received on-the-spot invitations for interviews for two of the five positions.

After making my way to each of the job sites, I left with a start date for both. I am very excited to have employment again. And, it will take both jobs to make ends meet, as both only pay slightly above minimum wage and are part time. My God always supplies.

Later this evening, I went to pick up a pizza to take over to my son and my niece and nephew. My plan was to sit and eat with them and to share the good news with my son about more money coming our way. Just as I was getting out of my car to head up to my sister-in-law's apartment, my cell phone rang. It was a good friend of mine asking me if I wanted to join him and his wife for dinner. I quickly accepted his invitation while running up the stairs.

While dropping off the pizza, I shared the good news about my two new jobs with my son before heading back out again. My son was so excited. He jumped up and down while hugging me tightly around my neck. He asked if we would be living together again soon. I told him to pray about it. Even though he is only eleven, he is a little prayer warrior. Both his mother and I always prayed at home and included him in our prayer time.

When I arrived to my friend's home, I shared the good news with him, and we hugged and praised God together. Eating a hot, home-cooked meal was very refreshing and welcoming, especially when sharing it with fellow believers. Before I left, my friend and his wife prayed with me, praying for both me and my son and our wellbeing. My heart leaped for joy.

As a faithful believer, Christopher walks in the boldness afforded him by the Lord. He is not timid when it comes to confessing and sharing his faith with others, even when he can tell they are not very receptive and want to avoid the conversation. Furthermore, he does not treat others unkindly when they do not share the same perspective or faith. This was exemplified when he spoke with the woman at the Employment Development Department. Despite the response of some individuals, Christopher believes the Word of God that says, "Some plant, some water, but God gives the increase" *(I Corinthians 3:6-8).*

Charles Spurgeon avowed, **"We have trusted in God, let us trust him still. He has never failed us, why then should we suspect him? To trust in man is natural to fallen nature, to trust in God should be as natural to regenerated nature. Where there is every reason and warrant for faith, we ought to place our confidence without hesitancy or wavering."**

PART THREE

*"Surely he shall deliver thee from the
snare of the fowler, and from the
noisome pestilence."*
Psalm 91:3

As the night grows later and morning nears, the temperature drops so low that I find it nearly impossible to stay warm even though I have several heavy blankets covering me. The cold chill causes me to go in and out of sleep. Each time I find myself awake, it takes about ten minutes before I can fall back asleep. At this moment, I am awake. But unlike the other two times I found myself awake, the night is not as still as one would expect it be at this hour. I hear dogs howling in the distance, as the sound of a fire engine fades away.

Out of nowhere, I hear the sound of trash crunching under someone's feet. Now, the door handle of my front car door is being tugged at. It's as though someone is checking to see if the door is unlocked, so he can gain entrance. The sudden intrusion is making me nervous as I realize my bladder is full and needs relief.

I really don't want to lift my head to see what is going on, but at the same time, I am unwilling to allow someone to take anything from me that the Lord has blessed me with. But, I'm not a fool. I will not place myself in harm's way. Neither will I give my life for material goods. And even if I didn't choose to live for myself, I have a son to raise. As I mentioned earlier, he is my sole responsibility.

Suddenly, as the door handle on the other side of the car is rattled, I am reminded of the verse, *"For God has not given us the spirit of fear, but of power, love, and a sound mind"* (II Timothy 1:7). From deep inside me, courage begins to swell up and overtake me. Slowly, I lift my head. Just as I do that, my face meets the face of the intruder.

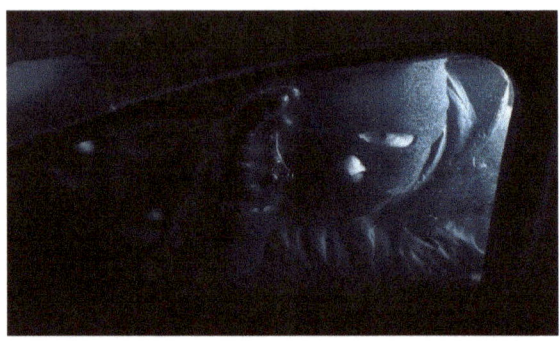

Suddenly, after our eyes meet, he turns and runs quickly down the street. He disappears so fast, I almost question if he was actually there at all. At that very moment, my breathing returns to normal, but I remain frozen in my spot. Maybe I think moving will cause the intruder's return.

After a few moments pass, I begin to thank God for His covering of safety. I realize the hedge of protection He placed around me is still intact. Therefore, the enemy cannot penetrate it without God's permission. Then, instead of opening the car door to exit the back seat, I climb from the back into the front and pull my keys from my pocket. Again, I'm using wisdom.

After starting my car, I drive slowly down the street, leaving danger behind me. Furthermore, I do not want to alert any police officers who may be driving by, so I act as though my being out at 3:30 in the morning is perfectly normal.

As I drive along, I am reminded of Job's plight. He suffered a horrible travesty when he lost all of his children in one day along with his earthly possessions. Then, to add fury to the devastation, he began to suffer in his physical body with boils covering him. He questioned God in an effort to understand what if anything he had done wrong. In the end, Job learned that his suffering was all for God's glory, demonstrating to Satan that he cannot turn the heads of God's children away from God and toward himself. God is going to be glorified in all the earth, and we are to sing of His praises.

Reflecting on Job, I realize God is not trying to punish me. However, He may be trying to get me to draw nearer and to trust Him in all situations without reservation. Whenever, I am faced with a challenge, I always stop and ask myself, "What is God trying to get me to understand?" I ponder this until the Holy Spirit reveals it to me. The answer does not usually come immediately. Most times, I don't get my answer until I have gone into prayer. When He does answer, I act accordingly.

God is always our refuge and our defender. No matter if danger attempts to find us or if we foolishly allow ourselves to become entangled in someone's web, God is always there to offer His assistance from the hand of the fowler- the wicked one.

Furthermore, the enemy himself is an evil spirit and engages with other evil spirits who do his bidding. God, who is the supreme spiritual being, can protect us from all evil spirits.

"He who is mysterious can rescue us from mysterious dangers; He who is immortal can redeem us from mortal sickness. There is a deadly pestilence of error, we are safe from that if we dwell in communion with the God of truth; there is a fatal pestilence of sin; we shall not be infected by it if we abide with the thrice Holy One; there is also a pestilence of disease, and even from that calamity our faith shall win immunity if it be of that high order which abides in God, walks on in calm serenity, and ventures all things for duty's sake. If all the saints are not so sheltered, it is because they have not all such a close abiding with God, and consequently not such confidence in the promise. Such special faith is not given to all, for there are diversities in the measure of faith. Too many among us are weak in faith, and in fact place more reliance in [this world system] than in the Lord, [the] giver of life. If we die of pestilence as others die, it is because we acted like others and did not in patience possess our souls" (Charles Spurgeon).

PART FOUR

"He shall cover thee with his feathers,
and under his wings shalt thou trust:
his truth shall be thy shield and buckler."
Psalm 91:4

Two weeks later, on a Friday, I was completing my first week of training for one of the two jobs I had been offered after visiting with the counselor at the Employment Development Department. After a full morning of learning soldering procedures and safety guidelines and taking a much-needed lunch break, I placed the safety goggles over my eyes and walked over to the soldering station. Mark, who was training me, lifted the iron, but he lost his grip. The iron fell, hitting the edge of the metal table, and bounced onto the floor- landing just half an inch from my left foot. Instinctively, I jumped back to protect my body from being burned. Both Mark and I had bewildered looks covering our faces.

Looking at my feet, I realized how blessed I am. My employer requires all workers, regardless of work station, to wear steel-toe shoes, and the company actually provides them on behalf of the employees. Unfortunately, I don't have mine yet. I went to the designated shoe store just two days ago, and my shoe size was unavailable. The store clerk placed the order for my shoes, but they will not be available for me to pick up until another four days.

19

Despite my dilemma, the employer allowed me to begin training, warning me to be careful.

So, as I looked at my feet, I saw a pair of old, worn-out Converse. The threads are beginning to show because I have worn them for quite a while. It is not as though I don't have other shoes. Most of them are in storage. I keep the Converse with me along with a pair of dress shoes for interviews, parent-teacher conferences, and other important business.

Tears fell quickly from my eyes, as I heard Mark's voice, coming seemingly out of nowhere. As if much time had passed, I was quickly shaken back to the time zone in which I was standing. Apparently, I had a blank look on my face. I had not heard what he had said. So, without even asking if I had heard him, Mark repeated his question: "Are you okay? Did the iron touch you?" Before I answered, I looked down again. Why I looked down is unknown even to me because I knew I had not been touched. I looked back up and softly, I whispered, "No."

Mark looked confused when he asked, "Why the tears?" Looking Mark directly in his eyes, I said, "They are tears of thankfulness. I'm thanking God because He shielded me from harm. These are just tears of joy." Mark nodded his head and patted my arm, demonstrating his understanding. We both understood that if I had been physically harmed, I would not have been able to continue working. Being unable to earn wages would only prolong my homelessness.

Mark, of course, does not know about my situation. But as a man who has his own family, he knows the importance and the value that is placed on a man providing for his loved ones and the honor connected to that. No man worth his salt is content to allow someone else to carry his load.

By the time I got myself together, Mark had retrieved the iron and had proceeded to complete the job we had started before lunch. Happily, I joined in.

For the first few moments, both Mark and I worked in silence. Then, Mark asked, "May I ask you a question?" Without lifting my head, I responded, "Sure."

Mark asked, "So, you are a Christian?"

"Yes, I am," I responded.

"That's comforting to know. I'm not really sure about others around here because I never hear a word spoken about God. So, it is sure nice to meet another believer."

"So, you've never said a word to anyone yourself?"

"Not lately."

"Why not?"

"Years ago, when I first started working here, I made a comment or two. You know, nothing too churchy. But, the other workers seemed to take a disliking to it, so I stopped. I didn't want to disturb the peace."

"Yeah, I understand. But, you do realize that is just what the enemy wants."

"What do you mean?"

"He wants to silence us. He doesn't want us to share the Good News of the Gospel. He wants us to be more concerned about our relationship with people rather than our relationship, love, honor, and respect towards God."

"Yes, but I must work, so I can take care of my family. A friend of mine was fired from his job because he insisted on telling someone about the Lord."

"God will give us wisdom about how to go in and out amongst His people without us being overbearing or pushy. Our beliefs may cost us some things, but God has formed a hedge of protection around His children. He will protect us."

"Are you saying you have spoken to people on your job and have not experienced any repercussions?"

"I speak to people everywhere I go, but I only do it with the leading of the Holy Spirit. I don't decide when I'm going to share. I allow the Holy Spirit to decide when He wants me to speak. And, when He tells me to speak to someone that is when I open my mouth."

"How do I know when the Holy Spirit is telling me to speak?"

"The Book of Revelation says repeatedly, *'Those who have an ear let him hear what the Spirit is saying.'* The more time you spend communing with God, you will begin to recognize His voice. He will speak to you and give you direction."

At that moment, both Mark and I were standing still. Without even realizing it, we had stopped working as we engaged in our conversation. Looking around and taking in the quietness of the shop, Mark said, "That sounds awesome. Maybe, we can grab a bite after work, so we can talk more about it."

"Sounds great," I responded, "but not today. I need to pick up my son from school."

"No worries. What day would be a good day for you?"

"Maybe on Monday. I'll let you know."

As I drove from work and headed towards my son's school, the conversation with Mark played over and over in my mind. It always amazes me how God opens doors and provides us with opportunities to connect us with other believers. That connection can help to strengthen our resolve and our walk, by giving us accountability and by keeping us focused on His Word.

Notice how Christopher is faced with one challenge after another. Most of our lives are the same way. While we may not be faced with homelessness, joblessness, etc., we still deal with multiple challenges at one time. For example, we may be faced with a problematic supervisor, a health issue, and not having enough money to cover a necessary expense.

Regardless of the challenges we face, what is important is keeping a healthy attitude about them, realizing God is able to do anything but fail! He is our all in all, and He, and only He, can deliver us from them all. Psalm 34:19 says, "Many are the afflictions of the righteous: but the LORD delivereth him out of them all." *If we can trust God to move on our behalf in one area, we can trust Him in all areas.*

According to Charles Spurgeon, "Even as a hen covereth her chickens so doth the Lord protect the souls which dwell in him; let us cower down beneath him for comfort and for safety. Hawks in the sky and snares in the field are equally harmless when we nestle so near the Lord. His truth --his true promise, and his faithfulness to his promise, shall be thy shield and buckler. Double armour has he who relies upon the Lord. He bears a shield and wears an all surrounding coat of mail--such is the force of the word 'buckler.' To quench fiery darts the truth is a most effectual shield, and to blunt all swords it is an equally effectual coat of mail. Let us go forth to battle thus harnessed for the war, and we shall be safe in the thickest of the fight. It has been so, and so shall it be till we reach the land of peace, and there among the 'helmed cherubim and sworded seraphim,' we will wear no other ornament, his truth shall still be our shield and buckler."

PART FIVE

"Thou shalt not be afraid for the terror by night;
nor for the arrow that flieth by day."
Psalm 91:5

I'm just leaving Joe's Hamburgers, after enjoying an evening out with some of the guys from work. Mark asked me and a few others to go out for burgers and fries. Some were able to go while others headed for home. I didn't have to pick up CJ from school today because this is the day my sister-in-law is off, so she picks up all the children and takes them skating.

This was the first time since Mark and I had our "spiritual" talk at work that we were able to go out. After everyone had finished eating and shooting the breeze about work, they began to head out one by one. Most of the dinner conversation circled around me, being the new guy, and how I was enjoying the job. Not knowing who was who and the relationship anyone may have with the boss, I kept my comments upbeat and cheerful, not that I have anything negative to say anyway.

After the last person left, Mark asked, "Where do you worship on Sundays?" I told him about my church that I have been a member of for thirteen years. He asked, "Did your wife go there too?" I told him she did and that is actually where we met. He nodded his head and added, "My wife and I go to different churches. When we met, we had already been members of our own church for quite a while and never altered our individual practices for worship service."

"Does that bother you?" I asked.

"No, it works for us. I know other couples who have struggled with the spiritual aspect of their lives, but we have been able to manage ours, and I'm thankful."

"You mentioned you have a son."

"Yes, actually I have two sons, fourteen and sixteen, and a ten-year-old daughter."

"So, where do the children worship, with you or your wife?"

"Both. Sometimes, they go to church with me and other times they go with my wife. We let them decide and do not pressure them about which one to go to. Sometimes, I also go to my wife's church and sometimes, she comes to mine. It all works out great."

"With all couples have to worry about today, where to worship shouldn't be a huge debate."

The conversation went from one vein of worship service to another. Mark shared with me the next event the men's department at his church is hosting and invited me to join them. I said I would, and I would bring my son with me. He nodded his head in approval.

"You think you will invite some of the other guys from work?" I asked.

"I doubt it."

"Do you mind if I invite some of them?"

"No, I don't mind. All they can say is no."

"Exactly. And, don't worry, I won't be overbearing. No one will look at you differently from just getting an invitation. Either they will come or not. It's okay to be an inviter." Again, Mark just nodded his head as he pondered my words.

After our goodbyes, we head in opposite directions. I spot a convenience store at the end of the block. I had been there before, and I vaguely remembered them selling fresh popcorn from their popcorn machine. Before going to sleep tonight, I want to see CJ and wrap my arms around him. I never go a day without seeing my son and telling him I love him. Tonight will be no different.

As I walk into the door of the store, the aroma of popcorn permeates my nostrils, and I breathe in deeply. It smells like the right amount of butter and salt on the kernels. I walk up to the counter and order two bags. The young lady behind the counter smiles brightly as she takes my order. While she is filling five bags, I wander to the back of the store to grab a six pack of ice tea. Then, I hear a deep, muffled voice say, "Empty the cash register."

The cashier screams, and the voice yells, "Shut up. I'm not going to hurt you. JUST GIVE ME THE MONEY!!!!" She begins to cry and panic. I lift my head from the cooler and look directly at her. I place my finger over my lips, signaling for her to be quiet. Seeing me seems to calm her down. She begins to follow the guy's orders, filling his bag with money from the register. After she is done, she hands it to him, with tears still falling from her eyes. He grabs it and rushes from the store.

The young lady continues to cry as she holds onto the edge of the counter. At that moment, her brother comes from the back and sees her panic. Quickly, he reaches under the counter and grabs a pistol and aims it at me as I walk toward them. I stop abruptly and lift my arms with the six pack in one hand. The girl manages to scream, "No!"

Her brother looks at her very confusedly. "What's wrong? What's going on here? What did you do?" he yells at her and me.

I don't utter a word. I don't want to say the wrong thing and end up as a casualty. The young lady says, "We were robbed. He went that way," as she points toward the door.

Her brother runs toward the door with his gun pointing forward. But, of course, the guy is long gone. I continue walking toward the counter, as I ask, "Are you going to call the authorities?"

She stops crying long enough to roll her eyes and say, "For what? They aren't going to do anything. We have been robbed before. That is why my brother keeps the gun under the counter. I'm afraid to use it though."

At that moment, her brother walks back in and asks me if I saw what happened. "Yes, I saw it all."

"Can you describe this guy?" he asks.

"Sure, he was a white or Latino guy wearing a black ski mask, and he had on a black leather-like jacket, a pair of black steel-toe boots, and blue jeans. He was about six feet tall. And, he was holding a nine millimeter."

"Is that right?" he asks his sister, turning his head in her direction.

"I guess so," she answers.

"What about his shirt?" the brother questions.

"I couldn't see it," she answers. He looks at me, and I just shrug.

Without saying another word, he walks around the counter and hugs his sister, who is still visibly shaken. He comforts her as only a brother can, as she melts into his arms, leaning her head on his shoulder.

Once I leave the convenience store, I have an opportunity to take a deep breath. And immediately, I begin to thank God for His net of safety that covers me day and night. I drive quietly to see my son with the free popcorn and ice tea in tow, thinking about how things could have easily gone differently. Like my wife who died at the hands of an intoxicated driver, I could have died at the hands of an angry gunman, leaving my son parentless. Shaking my head to rid myself of the disparaging thoughts, I focus on the drive ahead.

When I get there, my son, niece, and nephew are excited to receive the treats. My sister-in-law and I enjoy the now cold popcorn along with the children. In code, I tell her about the robbery while the children watch a movie. She shakes her head as she listens, while popping kernels of popcorn into her mouth. The look in her eyes resembles one of someone watching a mystery show, except there is no mystery. Just the hard, cold reality of life in the world we live in. Like me, she is thankful that I am safe and wasn't harmed.

Another day, another trial. Christopher managed to escape danger once again. This time, the danger was not directed towards him, but anything could have gone wrong in a moment's notice. Have you heard the phrase, "being in the wrong place at the wrong time"?

In this case, Christopher was in the right place at the right time. His presence probably saved the life of the cashier because she was in panic mode and could not think straight. Christopher was able to calm her down with one simple motion. If he were not there, anything could have happened. She could have panicked further and possibly got shot. Then, her brother, hearing the gunshot, would have rushed out, placing himself in danger. Who knows what could have transpired next?

As a believer, Chris was able to allow the peace that resides in him to control the dangerous situation he found himself faced with. That peace assisted in his aid to the young lady. This demonstrates that the peace of God comes to our aid, not just for ourselves, but also for those around us.

Charles Spurgeon commentates, *"Such frail creatures are we that both by night and by day we are in danger, and so sinful are we that in either season we may be readily carried away by fear; the promise before us secures the favourite of heaven both from danger and from the fear of it. Night is the congenial hour of horrors, when alarms walk abroad like beasts of prey, or ghouls from among the tombs; our fears turn the sweet season of repose into one of dread, and though angels are abroad and fill our chambers, we dream of demons and dire visitants from hell.*

Blessed is that communion with God which renders us impervious to midnight frights, and horrors born of darkness. Not to be afraid is in itself an unspeakable blessing, since for every suffering which we endure from real injury we are tormented by a thousand griefs which arise from fear only. The shadow of the Almighty removes all gloom from the shadow of night: once covered by the divine wing, we care not what winged terrors may fly abroad in the earth. Nor for the arrow that flieth by day.

Cunning foes lie in ambuscade, and aim the deadly shaft at our hearts, but we do not fear them, and have no cause to do so. That arrow is not made which can destroy the righteous, for the Lord hath said, 'No weapon that is formed against thee shall prosper.'

In times of great danger those who have made the Lord their refuge, and therefore have refused to use the carnal weapon, have been singularly preserved; the annals of the Quakers bear good evidence to this; yet probably the main thought is, that from the cowardly attacks of crafty malice those who walk by faith shall be protected, from cunning heresies they shall be preserved, and in sudden temptations they shall be secured from harm.

Day has its perils as well as night, arrows deadlier than those poisoned by the Indian are flying noiselessly through the air, and we shall be their victims unless we find both shield and buckler in our God. 0 believer, dwell under the shadow of the Lord, and none of the archers shall destroy thee, they may shoot at thee and wound thee grievously, but thy bow shall abide in strength. When Satan's quiver shall be empty thou shalt remain uninjured by his craft and cruelty, yea, his broken darts shall be to thee as trophies of the truth and power of the Lord thy God."

PART 6

"Nor for the pestilence that walketh in darkness;
nor for the destruction that wasteth at noonday."
Psalm 91:6

Now, two and a half months after beginning my two new jobs, I am looking forward to transitioning once again. However, this time, I'm going to allow it to be a surprise for CJ. It's a Sunday, and normally, I would be in worship service, but between the two jobs, Sunday is my only full day off. So, I must take care of this personal business today. Plus, Mark and Ted, another co-worker, are also free today, so I have to take advantage of their free time. Otherwise, I would have to pull off a solo act.

Right now, they are following me to my storage in Ted's pick-up truck, as I drive a U-Haul moving truck. I have a smile on my face and joy still resides in my heart. Once we reach my storage unit, it's all hands on deck. We are three men who are not afraid of hard work, which is a good thing because that is what awaits us.

We unload the unit and load the U-Haul in about an hour, arranging and rearranging, until mostly everything fits. The residual items are placed in Ted's pick-up. Finally, we are off to my new home, as I smile all the way.

Arriving at the new duplex apartments, my eyes light up as if though I have never seen them before. I see other families moving in also. And, they seem just as happy as I am. I see children bouncing about and making new friends. For a moment, I almost wish I had brought CJ along with me, so he could join in the fun with the other children and share in the excitement of making this place our home. However, I really want him to be surprised the first time I bring him here, and I want to set up his room for him, so he can just walk in and make himself at home.

When I saw the advertisement for this place, I didn't really think it would be a good fit for us- price wise. The advertisement did not include the price, which I thought was odd. And from the décor, both inside and out of the units, I assumed the rent would be out of my price range. But, I felt a tugging in my spirit to check it out anyway. So, I went to inquire, being prepared to leave and go elsewhere. I had a list of three other potential apartments in my pocket. But, upon arriving to the location and speaking with a rental agent, I was happily shocked.

The monthly rent was $50 below the amount I had set in my mind to not exceed. I was blown away. I couldn't believe I was being offered a new apartment with stainless steel appliances and granite counter tops in the kitchen and both bathrooms for an affordable price. In my excitement, I praised God as I reached for an ink pen. While looking around the promotional unit, I made the decidion to sign the rental contract the same day, without looking elsewhere.

Although it seems like a long time ago, it was only one week ago. And, it has been extremely hard to keep the secret from CJ. I consider myself good at keeping secrets and having the ultimate "poker face," but my excitement has not gone unnoticed by CJ or others I have come in contact with.

Twice, when CJ and I were out having an evening together, my mind would wander off in the middle of a conversation. He would say something to me, and I would miss complete sentences. He would have to shout, "Dad," to gain my attention. Smiling and snapping out of my daze, I would look at him and simply answer, "Yes, son?"

Then, he would ask, "Dad, are you daydreaming?"

Still smiling, I would answer, "I guess so, son."

"What about?"

"I'll tell you soon enough."

"Why can't you tell me now? Are you keeping secrets from me, Dad?"

"Actually, I am. But, not for long. I have a surprise for you, and I really want to give it to you, but it's not ready yet. I will give it to you in a few days. Just hold tight."

Trusting me explicitly, CJ nodded his head and returned to eating his ice cream sundae, his favorite treat.

Over the last month, he has been becoming more and more anxious each additional day we spent apart. So, this transition is desperately needed for both of us. It will set us back on a pattern of bonding together. Although we haven't stopped that process, it seems to be in spurts rather than continuous. Visiting him at his aunt's home makes me feel like a divorced parent with visitation rights. And although I am extremely grateful to her, I do not want CJ to wear out his welcome.

After Mark, Ted, and I finish unloading the U-Haul, I order pizza to be delivered to us, so we can have a quick bite to eat. I eat quickly, and then, I find the boxes that go into CJ's room. I open box after box and place his clothing into drawers and in the closet.

Next, I load his toys into the toybox and place his books on shelves. The final touch is to add his lamp to his desk. His mother bought him that lamp not long before the fatal car accident. He uses it to study with, even when the room is sufficiently lighted by the ceiling light. Using the lamp had become a regular part of his homework routine.

As I'm moving around in CJ's room, I hear the guys cleaning up the pizza boxes, plates, etc. When I step into the hallway, Mark asks, "When are you picking up CJ?"

Glancing at my watch, I respond, "In about 30 minutes."

"Well, we are going to get out of your hair. At this stage, you are on your own," Mark said with a laugh. Ted nodded his agreement as he joined in the laughter.

"Oh, no worries. Thank you guys so much for lending a hand. You two made it fast and easy for me. So, I'll see you guys at work."

They head out to Ted's truck, and I stand there watching as they pull away. Then, I walk back inside, take a quick glance around, grab my own keys, and head out.

Life circumstances are beginning to turn around for Christopher and CJ. What a blessing to have the favor of God operating in one's life. The hand of God is definitely upon them. Notice that Christopher is not taking any of the glory for himself. He could walk in self pride and talk about the changes he made to due to working hard on two jobs, but he refrains from doing so. He reserves the glory for God regardless of the trials he has faced over the last three years and especially during the last six months.

We would all do well to remember Proverbs 3:5-6 that says, "Trust in the LORD with all thine heart; and lean not unto thine own understanding. In all thy ways acknowledge him, and he shall direct thy paths."

Using the wisdom of the Lord, Charles Spurgeon reminds us: "Famine may starve, or bloody war devour, earthquake may overturn and tempest may smite, but amid all, the man who has sought the mercy seat and is sheltered beneath the wings which overshadow it, shall abide in perfect peace. Days of horror and nights of terror are for other men, his days and nights are alike spent with God, and therefore pass away in sacred quiet. His peace is not a thing of times and seasons, it does not rise and set with the sun, nor does it depend upon the healthiness of the atmosphere or the security of the country.

Upon the child of the Lord's own heart pestilence has no destroying power, and calamity no wasting influence: pestilence walks in darkness, but he dwells in light; destruction wastes at noonday, but upon him another sun has risen whose beams bring restoration. Remember that the voice which saith 'thou shalt not fear' is that of God himself, who hereby pledges his word for the safety of those who abide under his shadow, nay, not for their safety only, but for their serenity. So far shall they be from being injured that they shall not even be made to fear the ills which are around them, since the Lord protects them."

PART SEVEN

*"A thousand shall fall at thy side,
and ten thousand at thy right hand;
but it shall not come nigh thee."*
Psalm 91:7

I am standing at the bottom of the stairs that lead up to my sister-in-law's apartment. There are butterflies in my stomach. I'm preparing to share the news with my son that last night was his final night living with his aunt and cousins. I'm excited for the changes God has brought about in our life. So, the butterfly effect that I'm experiencing is not nerves. Rather, it is pure adrenaline!

By the time I get to the top, my hand shakes as I prepare to knock on the door. Just as I lift my hand, the door opens, and my sister-in-law steps out. Because her head is down, as she sends a text message, she doesn't see me right away. She almost bumps right into me, and my presence startles her. Stepping back quickly and looking up, she smiles when she sees it is me. She embraces me briefly and says, "He's in there," pointing to her bedroom. She, unlike my son, knows why I am there.

When I called to inform her that I was on my way, she had asked if I wanted her to pack CJ's clothes. I told her no because I didn't want anything to alert him of the news I had for him. Now, that I was there, he and I could pack together.

As soon as I entered the living room, my niece ran over to me and hugged me tightly. Then, she yelled, "CJ, your dad is here!" CJ bolted from the room yelling, "Dad, come in here," as he turned to run back into the bedroom. Pretending to be offended, I said, "What? No hug for your ole man?"

Ignoring my feigned disappointment, CJ jumps up and down, as he points to the television. There was a trailer about a new movie that had just been released. "That's the movie I told you about, Dad!" He is giddy with excitement and his cousins share in his enthusiasm. "Can you take me to see it?" CJ questions.

"Sure, no problem," I say as I grab him for a hug.

"Can we come, too?" my nephew asks, looking up at me with his huge, brown, doe-like eyes.

"Yeah, can we come too?" my niece chimes in, not wanting to miss out on the current excitement.

Before I can answer, CJ says, "Of course, you can come." Then, both my niece and nephew look from me to CJ and back to me again.

"Well, the boss has spoken," I say. "So, I guess it's the three musketeers and me for a movie." At that moment, my sister-in-law steps into the room, probably wanting to know what all the hoopla is about. I add, "Unless your mom wants to go too," I say to my niece and nephew. Glancing quickly at their mother for a response, the kids ask, "Do you, Mom?"

She shakes her head and says, "No, you guys can go and have all the fun. I'll just stay home where it is quiet and kid-free." We all laugh at her response. I know how she is feeling. For the last several months, she had been tasked with looking after three children. The only free time she had was when they were at school, and most of that time, she was at work. So, a free moment to herself would be welcome at any time.

"I will pick them up on Tuesday after school and take them to the movies."

"Sounds good to me," she says, without reservation.

"CJ, let's get your things packed."

"Where are we going, Dad?" CJ asks, looking confused.

"Do you remember the surprise I told you about?"

"Yes."

"Well, it is time to go to it."

"Where is it, Dad?"

"Not too far from here; just on the other side of town."

"So, you want me to pack an overnight bag?"

"No, I think it will be better if we packed all your things."

"To go to the surprise?"

"Yes, son. We are going to our new home."

"Dad, really?"

I do not need to answer CJ's question. He knows instantly that I am telling the truth. Maybe, he feels it in his spirit. I don't know. I just know he begins to pack. Then, about five minutes later, he sits on the floor and does not move. I stop packing also to see what is going on. Looking at his face, I see tears in his eyes. "What's wrong, son?"

"Nothing, Dad. God answered my prayer."

"I know, son. He answered mine, too."

Without any further words, CJ and I finish packing, thank his aunt and cousins for their hospitality, and head out the door. Twenty minutes later, we pull up to our new home. CJ gasps when he sees it. "This is it, Dad?" he asks in disbelief.

"Yes, son. This is our new home."

"It's better than the last apartment," he says, looking the building over from the roof, to the steps, to the plush green grass that lies in front.

"Let's check out the inside," I prompt, anxious for him to see his room. We both grab bags from the car and walk up the steps and into the door. Probably without realizing it, CJ drops his bags on the floor and begins looking around. Slowly, he makes his way through the living room, to the kitchen, and to the hallway. Slowly, I walk behind him, watching each expression.

Finally, we end up in his room. He walks in very slowly and looks around. He sits on his bed, seemingly to test if it all is real. Then, he walks over to his desk and touches the lamp. At that moment, I know he is thinking of his mother, and my heart begins to hurt.

"May I do my homework, Dad?"

"Of course, son."

He walks back to the front door, picks up his backpack, pulls out his homework, and sits at his desk. And, I leave him to it and go to my room to prepare for bed.

Christopher and CJ have faced great challenges that could have affected not only their mental stability but also their level of faith. If they had weak faith, the challenges could have overwhelmed them to the point where their faith was crushed completely, making it nonexistent. However, in the seven

excerpts you read, Christopher and his son demonstrated strong faith. Not once did their faith waver. Not once did they demonstrate doubt in God's ability, care, concern, or love for them. They knew, without a shadow of doubt, that God would come through for them, no matter the obstacle or circumstance they faced.

The response to their strong faith is well demonstrated by God in His method of deliverance. He stood by them and led them to safety. He also filled Christopher with encouragement and peace, so he was able to minister to others even while he was facing his own trials.

If we study the book of Job, from the beginning of the book to the end, we will witness how God used the needs of Job's friends to turn Job's attention away from his own problems to focus on theirs. Once he did that, he began to pray for their needs- albeit they may not have been aware they had needs. Meanwhile, God began to restore- double fold- all the enemy had stricken.

Like Job and Christopher, we all face trials at different intervals in our life. With strong faith and the hand of God, we can navigate through any challenge. Remember, we may not be able to handle all our problems on our own, but Matthew tells us in 19:26, "With men this is impossible; but with God all things are possible." So, rather than attempting to operate in our own physical, mental, or emotional strength, we should rely on the Almighty. He is the Omniscient One and the all sufficient one. In Him is all sufficiency.

Furthermore, God promised us in Isaiah 55:11 that His Word would not return unto Him void (unfulfilled). Rather, it will accomplish that for which it has been sent. Like Christopher, we can stand on the promises of God without wavering and without doubt, for the God we serve is faithful to His own word, for He is not a man that He should lie (Numbers 23:19).

Gift of Salvation
for Non-Believers

"For all have sinned, and come short
of the glory of God."
(Romans 3:23)

This section was written especially for non-believers, those who have not accepted the gift of salvation. The gift of salvation saves souls from eternal damnation and is a free gift offered by God Himself.

John 3:16-18 says, *"For God so loved the world, that he gave his only begotten Son, that whosoever believeth in him should not perish, but have everlasting life. For God sent not his Son into the world to condemn the world; but that the world through him might be saved. He that believeth on him is not condemned: but he that believeth not is condemned already, because he hath not believed in the name of the only begotten Son of God."*

This section of scripture tells us God's purpose for giving His son Jesus to the world. The world was in a bad condition. The world was overwrought with sin; the people were living for fleshly desires rather than for God's desires.

As a result of the world's conditions, God decided He would offer the perfect sacrifice that would save the world from being a place where people were lost and had no hope. He decided that His own son could stand in proxy for the sin-filled world, taking all sin upon Himself.

So Jesus came, born of a virgin, to save this dying world. He walked on this earth for 33 ½ years, doing the work of His Heavenly Father. At the appointed time, He died by way of crucifixion upon a cross at Calvary, on Golgotha's hill. He shed his blood and died for you and for me. Because His blood was pure, it paid the penalty for all unrighteousness and gave those who believe in Him direct access to His father's throne.

Scripture tells us in Matthew 27:51 that the veil of the temple was ripped in two from top to bottom, at the moment that Jesus' spirit left His body. As a result of the veil's removal, we are no longer required to have a high priest make intercession for us. We, as the children of the Most High God, are able to approach the throne of God for ourselves, and Jesus sits on the right hand of the Father making intercession for us.

But what is even more miraculous than God offering His own son as the perfect sacrifice was the fact that when Jesus was placed in grave clothes and placed in a tomb, He only remained there until the third day. God would not have it that His son would remain in the heart of the earth forever. In order for people to believe in the awesome power of God and His dear son Jesus, a miracle had to be performed. So, on the third day, after Jesus died on the cross, He was resurrected, demonstrating the omnipotence of God. This very act was the act that would cause people to believe in a god that reigns supreme and holds the power of the universe in His very hands, a god that could save them from themselves.

Today, if you are an unbeliever, you can change your destiny. You can change where you will spend your eternity. Our Heavenly Father gives us the freedom of choice about how we want to live our life here on earth and how we want to spend eternity. In Deuteronomy 30:19, God boldly declares, "*I call heaven and earth to record this day against you, that I have set before you life and death, blessing and cursing: therefore choose life, that both thou and thy seed may live.*"

So, dear friend what choice will you make today? Will you spend your eternity with the Creator or will you suffer Hell's eternal flames? Again, the choice is yours. Just as the men aboard the ship who were with Jonah became believers, you too can make a choice to accept the only one and true living God as your god.

If after reading the above passages, you have decided that you want to spend your eternity in Heaven with God, the creator, and His son Jesus, and the Holy Spirit, read through what has affectionately come to be known as the Roman's Road. This is the road to salvation. As you read through the scriptures that comprise the Roman's Road, you will also read the explanation for each scripture so you will have clarity about what you are reading and confessing.

The Roman's Road to Salvation

The road to salvation begins with Romans 3:23 which declares, "*For all have sinned, and come short of the glory of God.*" This scripture explains that everyone has come short of God's glory and needs redemption. Then Romans 6:23a states, "*For the wages of sin is death.*" Here, we learn that the consequence of living a life of sin is death. Everyone will experience physical death as a result of the sin committed in the garden of Eden, but those who commit themselves to a life of sin will suffer eternal damnation in the lake of fire (Rev. 19).

Continue with the rest of verse 6:23 that says, "*but the gift of God is eternal life through Jesus Christ our Lord.*" There is an alternative to suffering eternal damnation. We can accept the gift of salvation by accepting Jesus as our personal lord and savior. Then, Romans 5:8 says, "*But God commendeth his love toward us, in that, while we were yet sinners, Christ died for us.*" We are able to receive the gift of salvation because Christ came to earth and shed His blood for us on the cross.

Continue to Romans 10: 9-10 which says, "*That if thou shalt confess with thy mouth the Lord Jesus, and shalt believe in thine heart that God hath raised him from the dead, thou shalt be saved. For with the heart man believeth unto righteousness; and with the mouth confession is made unto salvation.*" If we confess with our mouths that Jesus is the son of God, that he came and died for our sins, and that God raised Him from the dead, we will receive salvation.

Finish with Romans 10:13, which states, "*For whosoever shall call upon the name of the Lord shall be saved.*" Call upon the name of God by saying these words, "Lord Jesus, come into my heart and save me Lord. I believe that you are the Son of God who came and died on the cross for my sins. I believe that you rose from the grave. I also believe that you now sit in heaven on the right side of the Father, making intersession for me. I accept you as my Lord and my Savior."

Now that you have confessed with your mouth that Jesus is the son of God and that He died for our sins and rose from the grave, YOU ARE NOW SAVED!!!! You will spend your eternity in heaven.

The next step is very important- you must find a Bible-based church that teaches the word of God and confesses the Lord Jesus Christ to be the son of God. Don't delay. Do this immediately. Do not leave yourself open to the enemy. Get connected with the saints of the Most High God and keep yourself covered with the unspotted blood of the lamb.

Here is my prayer for you.

Father God,

I thank you for the opportunity to minister your word to the unsaved, the unchurched, and the uncommitted. Father God, I pray now for the souls who have just received the gift of salvation. Lord Father, they have opened their hearts to you, and I know that you have received them into your kingdom and written their names in the Book of Life. Father God, I pray that you will touch their lives and show yourself mightily before them. Let their eyes be opened by the scales falling off, allowing them to see clearly.

Father God, I even pray for the backslider, those who have turned away from you after receiving the gift of salvation. You said in your word that you desire that none would perish. So Lord, I send your word to them right now praying that they would confess the iniquity in their heart, repent, and turn from their evil ways, so that they may receive a life of abundance. You said in your word in Matthew Chapter 14, that every knee shall bow before you and every tongue will confess that Jesus is Lord.

Father God, I pray now that we all come under subjection to your word and that we will humbly submit our lives to you. I ask all these things in the name of my Lord and Savior Jesus Christ.

Amen, Amen, Amen!!!!

I will continue to pray for your success in your walk with God. Remember, this spiritual walk that you are about to embark on will not be an easy walk, but remember, the race is not given to the swift but to those who endure to the end.

Be blessed with heaven's best. I love you!

About the Author

Dr. Cassundra White-Elliott resides in California with her family, where as an English/Education professor she works for various community colleges and universities.

When writing, she writes with the direction of the Holy Spirit, in an effort to share with God's people all that He has for them.

In addition to teaching and writing, Dr. White-Elliott also serves as an evangelistic teacher. She is also the founder of International Women's Commission, a ministry that serves the needs of the entire person, by attending to healing the mind, body, soul, and spirit.

Dr. White-Elliott holds a Ph.D. in Education, a Master's in English Composition, and a Bachelor's in Education.

Dr. White-Elliott is also the founder of CLF Publishing, LLC. For your publishing needs, go online to www.clfpublishing.org.

OTHER BOOKS BY THE AUTHOR
(All books can be purchased at
www.creativemindsbookstore.com)

***From Despair, through Determination,
to Victory!***

A lot can happen during a span of 40 years. The life of Dr. Cassundra White-Elliott has been anything but uneventful. From a fun-loving childhood sprinkled with incidents of abuse to a tumultuous young adulthood to a stable, secure adult life, she has experienced a full life, with much more to come. Her story is inspiring and motivating.

If anyone lacks hope, reading Dr. White-Elliott's autobiography will propel him/her into an attitude of "Maybe I can." This attitude, if nurtured and developed, will grow into an attitude of "Yes, I can." Throughout her life, Cassundra has always held in her heart the belief that she could achieve anything that she had a made-up mind to embark upon. She was determined to achieve her heart's desires, doing what God has called her to do. She takes no credit for herself. All the glory goes to God, for He is her driving force. In Him, she lives, moves, and has her being.

Through the Storm was duly inspired by the avaricious cloud of depression that decided to hover overhead of my daily existence in the latter part of 2007. Although I found it extremely difficult, I was once again compelled to not be defeated by just another snare that the enemy, the trickster, set for me. Once again, or more appropriately I should say *continuously*, he has exerted pernicious efforts to snatch the very life out of me by causing me to wallow in despair and to believe that I had been overcome by failure when in actuality and all reality, I was just experiencing a temporary setback. During those cloudy days, I had to remind myself daily that even though I was a target of the enemy, I am and will always be a child of the Most High god, Jehovah, who is my rock, my stability.

As I prepared to embark upon the adventure of writing this book, I had to prepare myself to also be transparent. I have found that being transparent is required in order for healing to transpire, healing for all those that peruse the pages of this book and myself. And I may as well tell you that today, at the onset of this project, I have not been totally delivered from my condition of being an anger-filled person. However, I am definitely a work in progress. I have made strides with the assistance of my Lord and Savior, Jesus Christ, who is the head of my life. Without his love, guidance, and teachings, I would not be the woman of God I am today. I shudder to think where I could be instead and will therefore not entertain the thought.

Chapter Two
How Communication Works
Purpose: This chapter will explain the six primary components of communication, identifying their purpose and how they work together.

The Source

In oral communication, the source of information is the speaker. In a church setting, the foundation of the message is God's word, but it is a speaker's interpretation of God's word that is delivered to the audience. As speakers vary, the information may vary but should have a similar essence because the foundational text is the same.

The Message

The message is the collective set of ideas that the speaker (the source) wants to deliver and/or illustrate to the audience.

Introduction

Where is Your Joppa? was written for the express purpose of illustrating God's call for obedience in the lives of believers with respect to the individual call that He has on each of our lives. As you read throughout the various chapters, notice that the emphasis is placed on our persistent disobedience in answering God's call in a specific area of our lives. We have become a people who are similar to the Israelites when they found themselves in the middle of the wilderness, following their exodus from Egypt. Before God, they murmured and complained about their current life conditions and failed to be obedient to God's statutes delivered through His servant Moses. Their persistent disobedience caused them to lose the opportunity to see and enter the Promised Land. I ask you, "What has your disobedience cost you?" "Was your disobedience worth what it cost you?" "Do you think about the souls you could have ushered into the kingdom of God?" These are some of the questions that I pray will be answered through your reading of the book.

Romero and Yolanda optimistically plan for the day that is going to change their lives from being single persons to a couple who is united in holy matrimony. They, along with their parents, close friends and family, fly over to the infamous Hamptons, where only the rich and famous vacation, to have their dream wedding at the five-star Hampton Suites located on a peninsula in the Hamptons. Little do they know that their perfect day will turn out to be less than perfect when their wedding planner Mariesha Coleman suddenly goes missing!

A time when the newlyweds' lives should be filled with joy and the creation of wonderful memories, they are stricken with grief as they desperately try to find clues to help solve Mariesha's disappearance.

Mayhem in the Hamptons is a tale that shares how the horrors of a woman's past can come back to haunt her in more than one way and the impact it can have on anyone who gets in the way.

Tinisha, the daughter of a preacher, is a twenty-six year-old God-fearing young woman endeavoring to complete law school so that she can make her mark in the courtroom. Working in one of the late-night clubs in Hollywood to earn money to pay her own way through school, Tinisha soon learns that life doesn't always go as planned.

Romero Turner is a private investigator with a promising future. As he continues to build his career, he is excited about the cases he undertakes. However, his father Pastor Theodore Turner has other plans for his son's life. In the midst of trying to save his client's husband from Sylvester Domingo, a ruthless crime lord, Romero must try to salvage his relationship with his father. He must decide if ministry or life as a detective is in his future.

Lord, Teach Me to be a Blessing! will change a person's mentality from being centered around "me, myself, and I" to focusing on "others."

The world system teaches us that it is acceptable to place ourselves above others in an attempt to get ahead and even to survive. Herbert Spencer coined the phrase *'survival of the fittest'* after reading Charles Darwin's theory of evolution. This concept of surpassing and outdoing others is the world's philosophy.

However, the word of God does not subscribe to or promote this self-centered ideology, and therefore, neither should believers. We must hold fast to the truths outlined in Scrip-ture: *"Love thy neighbor as you love thyself."*

Throughout the journey of life, we all experience ups and downs and joys and pains. Most of us successfully find solutions to the situations/problems we encounter, but we often avoid dealing with the attached emotions. If we continue to ignore the emotions of pain, hurt, disappointment, anger, etc., we set ourselves up for destruction. Our families, our cultures, and our society tell us to be strong, to keep our chin up, and to grin and bear it. However, these methods of avoidance can lead us to strokes due to the undue amount of pressure we place on ourselves and/or mental illness from being unable to cope with the emotional baggage we have accumulated.

A Diamond in the Rough

A Diamond in the Rough Architecture Firm was built and is owned and operated by lead architect Kyra Fraser. For the last five years, Kyra has been extremely successful in business, but her love life leaves much to be desired.

Kyra has set high standards for herself and does not wish to take a man in any condition and attempt to make him over. She is looking for someone who is drama free, well educated, very cultured, fun-loving, good looking, self-motivated, and the list goes on.

Will Kyra find the man of her dreams, or will her dream just continue to be a dream?

As you delve into this page-turning novel, Kyra's reality will unfold as you are drawn into her world of design, love and office drama- which includes her best friend's husband who is looking for love in all the wrong places.

Just as our brain requires oxygen obtained from the air we breathe to sustain our mortal bodies, our spirit requires revitalization and encouragement in order to be strengthened each and every day of our lives. The revitalization and encouragement needed for the spirit of man comes directly from the word of God and assists us in walking according to the way of our heavenly Father. 365 Days of Encouragement provides a scripture a day for each day of the year. Along with the daily scripture is a brief note of commentary also for the benefit of edifying the saints of God.

It is my prayer that the people of God would live a fulfilled life through Christ Jesus. Knowing His word and understanding we can walk in the fulfillment thereof is empowering.

A Mother's Heart

A Mother's Heart shares the unconditional love of mothers through a compilation of testimonies. Each testimony serves as a tribute to a special mother. The children of the represented mothers have lovingly written about their childhood, young adult life and/or older adult experiences they shared with their mother. As you read the writers' reflections, you will feel the expressions of love exude from the pages.

Our advice to mothers is, "Be encouraged; the journey of motherhood may seem daunting at times and you may shed some tears, but your children will never forget the love you have shown them and instilled in them to share with others."

Broken Chains is an in-depth survey of five life-changing tragedies that can and will serve as chains to bind us if we are not watchful and mindful of their potential effects. In our lifetimes, we may all experience death of loved ones, sexual abuse, broken relationships, promiscuity, and sickness and disease. These everyday life occurrences can have detrimental effects on the remaining years of our lives and change our existence, unless we deal with them in a healthy manner.

Broken Chains not only brings to light the detrimental effects of five life-changing tragedies, but it also shares how anyone who experiences them can be healed and delivered from their effects.

Do you know anyone who has committed his/her life to Christ but has done something unseemly that you would never expect a Christian to do? How did you feel about that person or what the person did? Did you pass judgment? What if that person were you? How would you feel if you made a misstep and no one forgave you and instead began to treat you differently? How do you feel when you are judged for past mistakes or lifestyles that are no longer part of your life?

This book shares four true stories of Christians who have made missteps during their walk with God. The purpose is not to air their dirty laundry, but to demonstrate our humanness and our vulnerability. None of us are exempt from making errors and falling into sin. It can happen to any of us.

The Bottom Line is a detailed review of the Book of Job. Much can be said about Job's experiences with the loss of his children and wealth and the subsequent return of it all in mass proportions. However, the telling of Job's story in the Holy writ was not intended to focus on the return of his wealth. Instead, the focal point should be on the bottom line of the entire situation.

When you experience trials or tragedies in your life, do you tend to focus on the trial itself, the result, or the bottom line?

"What is the bottom line?" you may ask. The bottom line is the message God is sending regarding the situation.

The ongoing conversation about the value of a woman is presented from a different perspective in *The Power of a Woman*. Dr. Cassundra White-Elliott presents a biblical perspective of women and compares it to the worldview of both yesterday and today. This comparison seeks to illustrate God's intended purpose for His uniquely designed creation: woman. Dr. Elliott shares God's truth about pre-imposed limitations set by man versus the limitations God Himself set for woman in addition to the wealth of liberality He gave her.

Women, let's take the blinders off, lift our heads up, and march forward, side by side with men, and bring glory and honor to God! Take your rightful place with a gentle smile and grace and be who God called you to be!

If you possess habits and display characteristics that are unbecoming, debilitating, and hinder the desired progress in your life or that affect your relationships with others, Set Free will provide the steps you need to be healed and delivered, through the Word of God.

Deliverance is available to you! Claim your healing today and walk in victory!

Have you or someone you know ever felt alone, confused, or unsure about your walk with God or are you unsure of what being a Christian is all about? *Do You Know God?* is an excellent text for providing answers to many of your questions. This book introduces adolescents and young adults to God in addition to answer many of their questions about being a Christian. This book shares the testimonies of the trials and tribulations that other teens have experienced and how God prevailed in their lives. All the information that is shared on the pages of the book is based upon the Word of God and the scriptures are taken from the King James Version of the Bible. If you are interested in knowing more about God's Word or how to begin your Christian experience, this book is for you.

A Mother's Heart

A Mother's Heart shares the unconditional love of mothers through a compilation of testimonies. Each testimony serves as a tribute to a special mother. The children of the represented mothers have lovingly written about their childhood, young adult life and/or older adult experiences they shared with their mother. As you read the writers' reflections, you will feel the expressions of love exude from the pages.

Mothers may not be perfect, but they are definitely unmatched by any other category of person on God's green earth!

A Mother's Heart II shares the unconditional love of mothers through a compilation of testimonies. Each testimony serves as a tribute to a special mother. The children of the represented mothers have lovingly written about their childhood, young adult life and/or older adult experiences they shared with their mother. As you read the writers' reflections, you will feel the expressions of love exude from the pages.

The purpose of this book is two-fold. First, it honors those mothers who stood by their children through the trials of life and showered them with unconditional love. Second, the book is a source of encouragement for mothers who may feel inadequate and question whether or not they are actually suited for motherhood. Our advice to mothers is, *"Be encouraged; the journey of motherhood may seem daunting at times and you may shed some tears, but your children will never forget the love you have shown them and instilled in them to share with others."*

Mothers may not be perfect, but they are definitely unmatched by any other category of person on God's green earth!

The following authors are included in this compilation:
Edwin Baltierra, Shelia Bryant-Colbert, Jean Cedeno, Ilse Guadalupe Hernandez, Haley Keil, Haley King, Johnathon Lopez, Ronnette Moore, Allyson Marie Sanders, Lucas van den Elzen, Daron C. White, Ashton Wilson, Jessica Yslas, and Vanessa Zavala

CLF Publishing, LLC.
www.clfpublishing.org

Dr. Cassundra White-Elliott's books are available at:
www.creativemindsbookstore.com
www.amazon.com
www.barnesandnoble.com

ISBN 978-1-945102-02-6
90000

9 781945 102028

 The journey from adolescence through puberty to young adulthood can be challenging and quite disconcerting for the average young lady. The changes that occur both mentally and physically can be both confusing and uncomfortable. However, the outcome of the changes can be beautiful. What she will experience during this time in her life is simply a metamorphosis – taking off the old and embracing the new. The process is similar to that of an awkward caterpillar that overtime develops into a beautiful, graceful butterfly.

The topics covered in this book (puberty, self esteem, mental stability, goals, finances, and relationships) will assist young women (ages 15–23) in understanding the transformation they are enduring to prepare them for the life that lies ahead. After taking in the information, they will literally witness themselves evolve from princess to queen!

CLF Publishing, LLC.
www.clfpublishing.org

Dr. Casaundra White-Elliott's books are available at:
www.creativemindsbookstore.com
www.amazon.com
www.barnesandnoble.com

ISBN 978-1-945102-15-8

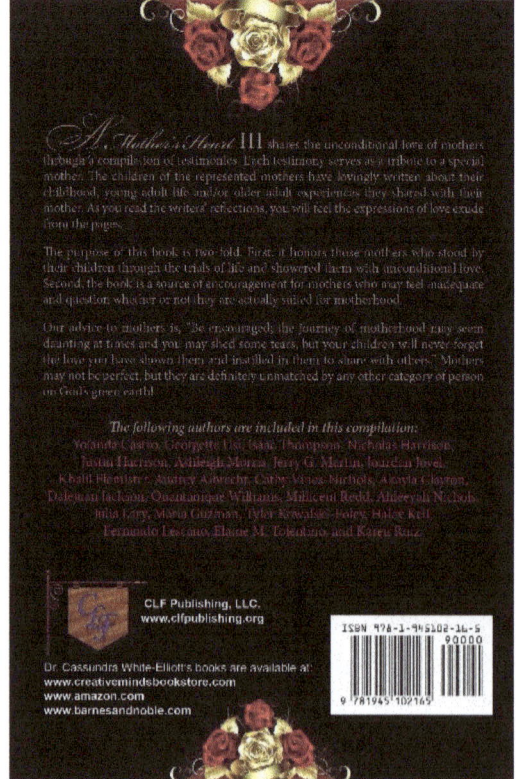

The Making of Dr. C. shares the 50-year journey of Dr. Cassundra White-Elliott. Her journey of trials, missteps, successes, and triumphs will inspire you to face any trial you may encounter with a positive attitude and the Word of God.

Her life demonstrates no matter what you may face, there is always a brighter tomorrow.

Keeping the faith will allow God to work in your life. After all, He only wants the best for you!

CLF Publishing, LLC.
www.clfpublishing.org

Dr. Cassundra White-Elliott's books are available at:
www.creativemindsbookstore.com
www.amazon.com
www.barnesandnoble.com

ISBN 978-1-945102-32-5
90000

9 781945 102325

Women's Study Bible

NEW INTERNATIONAL VERSION

Red Letter Bible

CLF PUBLISHING, LLC

Power of a Woman Series

CLAIM *Your*

INHERITANCE

Dr. Cassundra White-Elliott

"The thief cometh not, but for to steal, and to kill, and to destroy: I am come that they might have life, and that they might have it more abundantly" (John 10:10).

Satan's mission is to steal, kill, and destroy all that God has provided for us. With him on the rampage, we must be ready to go to war- spiritually and naturally. On the other hand, we could sit idly by and allow the enemy to take what is rightfully ours. However, that is not the will of God. God has given us power to tread upon serpents and scorpions (Luke 10:19) and to reclaim all the enemy has stolen from us.

This book will share how we can be victorious in reclaiming what is rightfully ours when the enemy has turned his ugly head in our direction and made us prey for his latest scheme.

With God on our side, the enemy will not prevail!

CLF Publishing, LLC.
www.clfpublishing.org

Dr. Cassundra White-Elliott's books are available at:
www.creativemindsbookstore.com • www.amazon.com • www.barnesandnoble.com

ISBN 978-1-945102-33-2
90000

9 781945 102332

January 2019

Christian Inspiration
A Publication of CLF Publishing, LLC

Other Interviews Inside:

Transforming Tragedy into Triumph

Weathering the Test of Time

Agape Koinonia Alliance

Red Carpet Ready Studio

Pastor JoEthel Kearney
Shaking Things Up For God!

www.ingramcontent.com/pod-product-compliance
Lightning Source LLC
Chambersburg PA
CBHW042145170626
46815CB00006BA/313